For my wonderful editor, Maria,
who discovered it's never too late to learn to splish splash!
—R.S.

Library of Congress Cataloging-in-Publication Data is available.
ISBN 978-0-06-197868-5 (trade bdg.) — ISBN 978-0-06-197869-2 (lib. bdg.)
Typography by Jeanne L. Hogle
11 12 13 14 15   LPR   10 9 8 7 6 5 4 3
❖
First Edition

Rob Scotton

Splish,
Splash,
Splat!

HARPER

An Imprint of HarperCollinsPublishers

Splat purred happily in his sleep as candy fish of all shapes and sizes swam through his dreams. He reached out to catch one . . .

when his mom threw open the curtains.
"Time to get up," she called.

The candy fish melted away.
"Come back, little fishes." Splat sighed.

"Oh, I almost forgot," said Splat's mom. "Spike's coming over for a playdate after Cat School."

"Spike! Spike! Spike!" spluttered Splat. "Spike will eat all the candy fish and play with my toys until they break."

"There will be plenty of candy fish, and we'll put away your favorite toys," said his mom. "Although . . . wouldn't it be nice if you shared?"

"Sure, with anyone but Spike," said Splat. "He's a show-off. He calls me names. AND he doesn't like me."

"I'm sure he really likes you," said Splat's mom. "Now get in the bath or you'll be late."

"But water is horrible," said Splat. "It's scary and wet and makes me soggy."

"And don't forget to wash behind your ears," said his mom.

A few seconds later . . .
"Finished," cried Splat.

"I think you missed a bit," said his mom.
"Aww!" said Splat. And with a SPLISH!
he lowered himself into the water.

"Oh, I almost forgot—you begin swimming
lessons at school today," said his mom.

"This is not going to be a good day,"
Splat said at breakfast.
Seymour shook his head.

"Not a good day at all," Splat said
on his way to school.
Seymour shook his head.

"Can this day get any worse?"
Splat asked.
Seymour looked through Splat's
legs . . . and nodded.

"Hi, Splattie! Last one to school is a loser," said Spike with a grin.

Spike sped through a puddle with a SPLASH! and was gone.
"What a show-off," said Splat. "This is definitely going to be
the worst day ever."

In class Mrs. Wimpydimple made an announcement.
"Today, class, we are going to learn how to swim."

The class fell silent . . . almost.

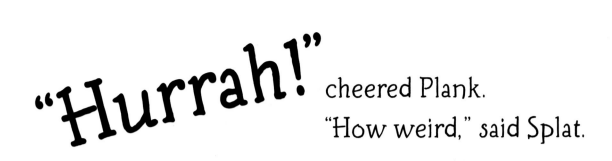

"Hurrah!" cheered Plank.
"How weird," said Splat.

"Class, to the *swimming pool!*" continued Mrs. Wimpydimple.

The class lined up by the pool.

NOT DEEP   GETTING DEEPER

"Splat forgot to put on his swim trunks," teased Spike.
Everybody laughed.

"No I haven't! They're black and furry," Splat replied.

"It's time to get into the water," said Mrs. Wimpydimple.

"Yippee!"
cried Plank.
And he jumped into the pool.

"That's really weird," said Splat.

"Me next," cried Spike.

Spike rushed up to the pool edge.
But then he stopped and stepped back.

"Hmm . . . I forgot something,"
he said.
Some of the class slowly
stepped into the pool.

"**Me next,**" cried Spike again. He rushed to the pool edge, but once again he didn't get in.

"I forgot something else," he said.

More of the class got into the pool.

Soon there were only two cats left by the side of the pool—
Splat and Spike.

"Come on in," said Mrs. Wimpydimple. "It's a lot of fun,"

Splat couldn't keep quiet any longer.
"Water is horrible!" he blurted, hiding
behind Spike.

"Yes . . . yes, it's horrible," said Spike,
hiding behind Splat.

"Water is scary . . . and wet!"

they cried together.

"And it makes us soggy."

Splat was confused.

He thought that Spike wasn't afraid of anything,
but Spike was just as scared as he was.

Splat felt sorry for him.

Splat looked at Seymour.
Aha! he thought.

Then Spike saw the strangest thing.
A candy fish floated in front of his face!
Spike tried to catch it. He missed.

He tried again and again but
still couldn't catch it.

Then he made one last effort
and finally . . . **"Yum!"**

Then Spike realized that he was standing in the swimming pool!
"How did that happen?" he wondered.

Hmm, it doesn't feel horrible . . . or scary . . . or too wet, thought Spike.
"Hey, Splattie, last one to the other side is a loser!"

If Spike can do it, so can I, thought Splat.
He took a deep breath and jumped.

SPLAT!

"Hmm, it tickles!" said Splat. "Water's not horrible at all."
Splat called to Spike, "Last one to the other side is a loser!"

Later that day Spike went over to Splat's house.

He ate lots of candy fish and played with
Splat's toys . . . but he only broke one.

He also gave Splat the perfect present.